THE
CINDERELLA
REBUS BOOK

retold by
ANN MORRIS
pictures by
LJILJANA RYLANDS

ORCHARD BOOKS
New York

ORCHARD BOOKS
387 Park Avenue South
New York, New York 10016

Orchard Books Canada
20 Torbay Road
Markham, Ontario 23P 1G6

Orchard Books is a division of Franklin Watts, Inc.

Book design by Jennifer Campbell

The text of this book is set in 18pt Rockwell Light.
The illustrations are black line colored pencil.

2   4   6   8   10   9   7   5   3   1

Library of Congress Cataloging-in-Publication Data

Morris, Ann, 1930–
The Cinderella rebus book.

Based on the fairy tale Cinderella.
Summary: A rebus version of the fairy tale about the
poor young girl who is helped by her fairy godmother, in
which pictures are substituted for some words or parts of
words.
[1. Fairy tales.   2. Folklore—France.   3. Rebuses]
I. Rylands, Ljiljana, ill.   II. Cinderella.   English.
III. Title.
PZ8.M8287Ci   1988   398.2′1 [E]   88-1451
ISBN 0-531-05761-5
ISBN 0-531-08361-6 (lib. bdg.)

Printed in Belgium

THE CINDERELLA REBUS BOOK

This story is a wonderful puzzle to solve! Words or parts of words are replaced by very small pictures, letters or numbers. Coach becomes , Prince becomes , ballroom room, are R and to 2.

If you can't work out the meaning of a word, just look it up in the rebus dictionary at the end. Here you will find a list of all the rebus words in the story in the order in which they first appear.

Then, if you look carefully, you can have fun picking out the tiny objects which are shown again in the big pictures.

Now read and Njoy *The* *Rebus* !

Once upon a time there were 3 sisters who lived in a 🏠 not far from the 👑's 🏰. The youngest, 👧, was pretty and loving, but the other 2 were ugly and proud. They were jealous of 👧's beauty and gentle ways. They were exactly like their mother, who had married 👧's father after his first wife died.

 had **2** do all the work in the 🏠 while the 👧👧 admired themselves in their elegant 👗👗 and 💎. She made the 🛏🛏, beat the 🧺🧺, scrubbed the floors and washed the 🫖. And it was always 👧 who tended the 🔥. In fact, she was called 👧🐝cause she was so often covered with cinders from the 🔥place.

At night 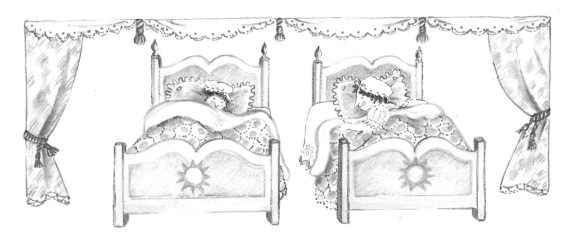 slept in the cold with nothing but and 4 company. Every morning she got up early while her 2 lazy slept soundly in their soft, comfy . But even though her nagged and scolded her all day long, was not unhappy.

Just 🐝 **4** Christmas there was **2** 🐝 a great 🍉 at the 🏰 for the birthday of the 👑's son. Invitations were sent **2** important people throughout the land. But, although invitations arrived **4** the **2** ugly 👭, they had made sure that 🧹 was not invited.

On the day of the 🍉 the **2** ugly 👭 spent hours and hours getting ready. 🧹 had **2** help them. As they squabbled over what they should wear, they scattered 👗👗 and 👡👡 and 📿📿 and 👱👱 all over the floor.

That night the streets were lit with bon🔥s and ✨. The country people were dressed in their best clothes and stood by 2 watch the lords and ladies as they drove off 2 the 🏰 in splendid 🚃🚃.

It was late when the 2 ugly 👧👧 finally left 4 the 🎃.

"👨, U can tidy our 🛏rooms," said 1 👧.

"And U can wait up and help us get undressed when we get back," said the other 👧.

And with that they were gone.

 was so tired she sat down in the 🏰 next 2 the flickering 🔥. In the distance she could hear the sound of music from the 🏰 2 cheer herself up she sang a little song she had learned from her mother.

 was just about 2 fall asleep when she heard a gentle knocking at the 🚪. She went 2 open it and looked out in2 the dark night. There stood an 👵 wearing a long 🧥 and a pointed 🎩.

"Good evening, m👁🦌," said the . "Y R U sitting here when everyone has gone 2 the 🎃?"

"👁 was not invited," said 👧. She did not know who the 👵 was but she felt she was someone special. "Please come in and warm yourself by the 🔥."

The 👵 hobbled inside.

"👧, 👁 am your 🧙," she said. "👁 can help U get 2 the 🎃."

👧 gasped. "But how can 👁?" she asked. "👁've nothing 2 wear but this ragged 👗."

"Just do as 👁 say, m👁🦌," said her , and she smiled.

From under her  the 👵 drew out a magic 🪄. She raised it into the air, and in a single moment 👧 was dressed in a beautiful 👗 all covered with 🎀 and 🌸.

"But 🧙, how can 👁 go 2 the 🎃 wearing these old 👟?" 👧 asked. The 👵 waved her 🪄 again and 2 👟 made of glass appeared 2 replace 👧's worn-out 👞. 👧 slipped her small 🦶 in 2 them.

Then  asked, "How will 👁 get **2** the 🎃?"

Her pointed **2** the 🎃 which stood in the corner of the room.

"Take the 🎃 outside, m👁 🦌," she said.

Once more she waved her . The 🎃
grew fatter and fatter. All of a sudden, there
stood a handsome 🚃.

With another wave of the ✦ the 🏠 🐭 🐭 were changed into **6** beautiful white 🐎 🐎 **2** pull the 🛺. Then her 🧙 changed the 🐀 🐀 into a 🛺 man and **3** 🦶 men.

"And now, m[eye][deer]," said the [old woman], "[eye] must leave U. But there is 1 thing U must [bee] sure 2 remember. U must [bee] gone from the [castle] [bee]4 the [clock] strikes 12. The [carriage] will [bee] waiting 4 U."

"Oh, [deer] [fairy godmother], how can [eye] ever thank U enough?" said [Cinderella].

Then she stepped in2 the [carriage]. The [carriage]man cracked his [whip] and they were off 2 the [castle].

When  entered the great ● room all

the 🎻🪗🎺 stopped playing and everyone

stopped dancing 2 stare at her.

"Who is she?" they all whispered.

The 👑 walked over 2 👸 and bowed

low. Then they danced together all evening.

Everyone wanted know about the young

girl who made the look so happy. Even

the ugly had no idea she was .

Suddenly  heard the great 🔔 of the

🏰 🕰 chime: **1**, **2**, **3** …

"What time is it?" she cried.

"It's almost midnight," said the .

 drew herself away and fled out in **2** the night as fast as her  would carry her. At the bottom of the  case she stumbled. **1** of her  flew off her . But the  was waiting **4** her and **4** she realized what had happened she was back again in her corner of the .

The [picture] had gone out and [picture] shivered with cold. She was dressed in her old ragged [picture] again, but she was still wearing a glass [picture] on 1 [picture]. All the magic was gone but [picture] had that 1 glass [picture] 2 remind her of the 1derful night at the [picture]'s [picture] when she danced with the [picture]. In2 the [picture] went the glass [picture] so that her [picture] would not C it.

At the [picture] the [picture], who had found the other glass [picture], looked everywhere 4 the beautiful girl who had won his [picture]. The [picture] said that he would give a reward 2 anyone who had news of her or of the [picture].

Messengers were sent from the **2** search **4** the beautiful stranger. Every lady in the land was asked **2** try on the glass **2** **C** if it would fit.

At last the messengers arrived at the of the **3** sisters. Each of the **2** ugly tried **2** force her in **2** the , but it was **2** narrow **4** the first and **2** short **4** the second.

"Do U have any other sisters?" asked 1 of the 's messengers.

"No! No!" shouted the 2 ugly . Yet, at that moment, faint singing could heard.

"Who is that?" asked the messenger.

"It was a little ," said 1 .

"It was the squeaking of a ," said the second .

The messenger went 2 C 4 himself. He found in the corner of the . When she saw the glass he carried, she smiled.

"**Y** do **U** smile, mchild?" asked the 🤴's messenger.

"🐝cause 👁 have a 👡 exactly like that **1** myself. It's in the 🪑🏺🐱🪑🛋️🧰." She brought it out and put it on with the other glass 👡. Everyone could **C** that they were a perfect fit.

Straightaway  was taken 2 the who was overjoyed 2 C her. He asked her 2 marry him. The and were delighted and treated her like a long lost daughter.

People came from far and near **2 C** the wedding of  and her . The most important guest of all was 's . When she arrived she was wearing her long , but she **8** nothing, drank nothing and said nothing. She just smiled and smiled.

As **4** the **2** ugly , they sat at home endlessly arguing with each other as the wedding 🔔🔔 rang out in the distance.

REBUS DICTIONARY

The rebuses in this dictionary are in the order

they first appear in the story.

3 three	rugs	
house	dishes	
King	fire	
palace	cause because	
Cinderella	place fireplace	
2 two, to, too	 kitchen	
sisters	rats	
dresses	mice	
jewels	**4** for	
 beds	**4** before	

be · green

ball · cape

slippers · hat

necklaces · m 👁 my

wigs · dear

bon 🔥 s bonfires · Y why

torches · R are

coaches · 👁 I

U you · Fairy Godmother

1 one · 👁've I've

🛏 rooms bedrooms · dress

door · wand

in2 into · gown

old woman · lace

pearls

 shoes

 feet

 pumpkin

 coach

6 six

 horses

 man coachman

 men footmen

 clock

12 twelve

 whip

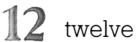room ballroom

 musicians

 Prince

 bell

 case staircase

 slipper

 foot

1derful wonderful

 cupboard

 see

 heart

 bird

 Queen

8 ate

 bells